Learn to read with
Posy the Pig

Words by Sue Graves
Illustrations by Jan Smith

book-studio

"I'm going to a party!" said Posy the pig.

"I'll look like
a pop star if
I put on a wig."

The pink wig
didn't fit.
It was too big.

"This wig is
too big."

"I'm sure I'll find my green wig if I dig and dig."

"Love the wig, Posy!"

The party was held in Sid Pig's rig.

For lunch, Posy ate a big, ripe fig.

Then, all the pigs danced to a band called Mig.

Posy won a prize for the best wig. She did a little jig.

"Your wig is the best!"

"Wow!" said Posy. "What a super gig!"

The end